Voice Lessons

and Other Poems

John Tynan

© 2010, 2015 by John Tynan
Book design © 2015 by Sagging Meniscus Press

ALL RIGHTS RESERVED.

Cover design by Royce M. Becker.
Set in Adobe Garamond with LaTeX.

ISBN: 978-0-9861445-0-9 (paperback)

Sagging Meniscus Press
web: http://www.saggingmeniscus.com/
email: info@saggingmeniscus.com

For Rene

my soul mate

and my love

and for our sons Miles and Sterling

Acknowledgements

With special thanks to those along the way who believed in me and in these words.

To my parents Chet and Gene Tynan; to my friends Manoog and Ia Hadeshian, Todd Mainey, Alex Thomas, Joe Loga, Bill Miley, Chris Bryson; and to my teachers Roger Stanley, Merle McPheters, Will Clipman, Judson McGehee, Arnold Johnson, Alan Woodman, Jim Simmerman, Becky Byrkit, Jane Miller, Jon Anderson, Boyer Rickel, Gibb Windhal and Steve Orlen; to my classmates and colleagues Glenn Levy, Deborah Bernhardt, Eric Burger, Michael Spurgeon and Karen Falkenstrom; to my fellow writers Rene Gutel, Rich Kenney, Shari Bombeck, Carol Hogan, Robin Lieske and Jennifer Waters; thank you for the indelible mark that you have left on my work and on my life.

Special thanks to Engelbert Gruber and Jacob Smullyan for their encouragement and their generous and invaluable contributions they have made to the printing of this work.

Contents

Change of Fortune · *1*

An Excellent Meal After Unprotected Sex · *2*

Yesterday's Geniuses · *4*

Checkout Line · *6*

Batters' Practice · *8*

I Know I've Wanted to be Here Before · *9*

All My Exes · *10*

Mixed Up Weather · *12*

A Golden Solution · *14*

Dog Among Icons · *15*

Exchange of Devotion · *16*

About Face · *17*

The Poem as Conduit · *18*

Certain Counsel · *20*

Love is the Soul of Genius · *22*

A Poem for Our Futures · *23*

Down On Weighted Knees · *24*

Prayer for Our Parents · *25*

206 Mill Street · *26*

Music Appreciation · *27*

Voice Lessons · *28*

My Papy's Hand · *30*

Our Last Defiant Days · *31*

The End of Mischief · *32*

The Leader · *34*

All Our Soiled Laundry · *36*

Two Statues · *37*

What Hollywood Wants from a Poem · *38*

Voice Lessons

Change of Fortune

Bonked off my bike by a snowbird from Maine
brought me thirty grand of windfall fortune
that came, after the lawyers took their take
and the doctors with their sterile torture.

Alive and lucky, it was just a long headache.
Then, a sudden interest in my future
led to a series of meetings and handshakes
with your average corporate baby boomers.

As in a dream vacation in Las Vegas,
where the pit boss takes you into the fold
of back rooms, secrets, and one-way glass,
you see – as chump change – your new-found bankroll.

A common Joe in the eyes of the bank,
you discover, once more, the wealth of poems.

Voice Lessons

An Excellent Meal After Unprotected Sex

Were you to have been conceived yesterday afternoon,
I would like you to know, my daughter or son,
that your first nourishment was duck à l'orange
served to a table of friends Howard, Katrina, your mother and I,
by a waiter named Roland and prepared to perfection by Chef Omar
    Matmati
in a restaurant named Fenix, in the city of its namesake.

Were you to have been conceived yesterday as the light in the blinds faded,
I would like you to know that the wind was brisk, and that your mother wore
a brand new, red striped, purple shirt from Urban Outfitters
with a wide, French collar and her hair in a tight bun flanked by two
    sparkling barrettes.

Were you to have been conceived yesterday afternoon, I would like you to
    know
that the first sparks of taste awakening in you were that of red Zinfandel
glinting off the flint of a few pepper grains ground by our waiter
over a plate of romaine lettuce lightly glazed in vinaigrette.

Were you to have been conceived in that blush of light,
I would like you to know that the first inklings of sight
that may have come down to you were a brilliant red
that your mother might have registered from across the table,
remarking that the shade of Katrina's scarlet eyeglass frames perfectly
    matched her dress.

Were you to have been conceived that afternoon, I'd like you to know
that your first impulses to question might have been shaped
by your mother prying Howard for his political bent
and your first feelings of satisfaction might have come as well,
as the question was carefully rewarded, like the opening of a salty shell,
when Howard revealed only enough to imply a larger, more interesting whole

than any of us would have guessed, given the evidence
that a few years of acquaintance had deceptively sketched.

Were you to have been conceived that afternoon, you might have have heard
the first tones of excitement in Rene's voice as she talked about her work,
a radio interview she held the night before with another in a long line
of quirky characters, you may have intuited the power
to extend a microphone forward in the world and extract truth,
through plain, intended talk and words of conviction.

Were you to have been conceived yesterday afternoon, I would like you to know
that I wore an emerald green sweater and a pair of new, staggeringly expensive, brown Naot shoes
which grew, over the course of the evening, remarkably comfortable.
I would want you to know that I mentioned to the other guests,
how earlier that day I attended a poetry workshop where I came away excited,
delighted from finding the right poem to explicate a particular topic,
and hopeful for the possibility of living an academic, writer's life.

You, who may have been conceived that afternoon, February 3rd 2007, I would like you to know,
your first hundred minutes in the world, your first glimpse of consciousness
coincided with the most excellent meal of my recent memory
and where, in those hours the restaurant staff allowed our conversation to unfold,
you were given a leg up on the finer points of friendship,
a head start on the art of smart, relaxed talk,
there, with your mother and I, and two good friends,
in the city where I learned to appreciate great eating.

Voice Lessons

Yesterday's Geniuses

One afternoon not long ago, I watched two men talking;
for half an hour they monopolized an aisle at the Goodwill Store
flanked on each side by typewriters and televisions, phonographs and radios
with illustrated lightning and radar echoes around the names
of models from the factories of Futuretron and Electro-Scope.

I imagine these guys are retired research assistants and ham radio buffs:
the neighbor with so many antennae on his roof
you would think he leased his house from NASA;
where late each evening the garage door windows cast an incandescent glow
into a dark, where the chirping of crickets
seemed almost like Morse code from halfway around the globe.

And I wonder about these Bakelite buddies,
about the tools and the ends of their work.
How their talk is similar to what you might hear today
listening to the technology segment on the news, a whole revolution
of acronyms, of dot coms and companies with names that sound
like synthetic elements in a fresh, new periodic table
cooked up for another generation of white-collar workers,
only to leave the fine ideas of their predecessors
as banged-up relics on a shelf in some thrift shop.

And I think about these one-time Mr. Wizards
and the echoes that they must sense in these discarded things,
the system of solutions and approaches each relic presents
and how important it is for these friends to assess – together –
these arrangements of spent vacuum tubes and banged-up metal.

Perhaps one of them had a friend, like I did,
a partner they had wished to work with for the rest of their life.
Perhaps they imagined a curious life spent building and planning
until, one day, they would open a shop of their own,

the culmination of discussions in restaurants and coffee shops,
their wives or girlfriends sitting nearby and rolling their eyes
at the unintelligible talk of transistors and who knows what.

Perhaps, on a midnight one of them cannot forget,
the other man's wife's voice through the telephone handset
saying that he was dead. What do you do then?
How much doubt and hurt goes into your work,
and will it ever be the same?

That's why I applaud these imagined heroes
for the filament of figuring things out that's radiating in their heads
and the resonance that comes from two friends sharing technical things.

Voice Lessons

Checkout Line

Last night, Nancy asked me to pick up some milk.
So I ambled the aisles of the ABCO eyeing the shelves
for food that would bring comfort to my life.
No visions of Whitman among the watermelons.
No great dismay over the hold that corporations
may have on my wallet, or the mind
that chooses Donald Duck over the Tropicana Girl.
Just another jamoke with a middle-manager's belly
bringing home the bacon to his suburban beauty.

Across the aisle, a couple with facial piercings and bikers' clothes
are goofing around as they decide
on just the right bakery item. They single out the whitest,
sweetest, frosted creation and carry it with a grin
to the checkout line, where a woman who treats each exchange
with the same feigned "How are you?"
punches in a late-night liquor sale
and a college coed's weekly run of frozen dinners.

The couple, looking like a pair of matted terriers,
step to the back of the line carrying the sheet cake between them.
They snicker at the juxtaposition of their black-booted, Gestapo selves
waiting in the middle of the supermarket like any ordinary, anybody else,
doing the bland old things that people do.

After, as I push my groceries out to the car,
chirp the remote for my leased Lexus,
and slide a carton of Almost Eggs onto the passenger seat,
I see the couple loading their pastry into the hatchback
of a beat-up Datsun, its surface plastered with slogans
like a hand-stamped steamer trunk

traveling through countries of Anger and Doubt,
and I think of the work that goes into maintaining an image,
the tactics it takes to be a part of a crowd.

Voice Lessons

Batters' Practice

an epithalamion

What has undoubtedly been a remarkable spring training,
a vast acceleration of their relationship,
in all this forward momentum, the bride and groom
would like us to take a moment, today, to pause with friends,
and have a conference on the mound,
with all of us in the stands, cheering!
And if I may be so foolish or so brave as to strain
the metaphor of America's favorite pastime past its breaking point
to find a corollary of baseball as a form
for marriage as evidenced in life,
I might think of it as a kind of question and answer game
to be played out on the ball-field
of a municipal park, a couple alone:
the husband lobbing softballs to the wife at bat,
and then the opposite. The woman pitching
and the husband's careful attention as he readies his bat in reply.
It's this kind of private practice
that improves individual performance;
this finding ways to fine tune and ratchet up
the average for the current season.
But you never hear about these kinds of pairs in the major leagues.
It's not the warm-ups that get the attention –
but the rare exceptions, the three runs batted in
after the 7th inning stretch to clinch the game.
But were they to give credit to the warm-ups,
to these daily tunings, these constant corrections
that might have carried a hitter across the range
of his (or her) better years, they would do good
to look to this simple husband's and wife's exchange,
these conscious, considered motions with each at bat.

I Know I've Wanted to be Here Before

The hammock, as seen past the French doors, sways in a lattice of shade.
The geometry between sitting and what's seen forms its own weight, a feng
    shui
that propels me through this morning's montage of reminders,
sets a particular tone, muses at the piano in a pedal point of intent.
And in that moment, it's almost as if the words have already been chosen
for the gestures and trajectory of the full span of the day.

And it is not so much a rarefied moment as it is deliberate.
Even the most mundane few minutes over the frying pan with a glob of
    breakfast sausage
fits into a larger plan; of perhaps, saving some dollars where you can say in
    three weeks time,
"I live better, due to this-saved-amount"; a number that has real relation to
    events and things,
a node in a web of intentions. And it all culminates in a kind of quality;
an intentional déjà vu where you might think, "I know I've wanted to be here
    before."

To pursue this quality of moment is to start each day at the center of your bed
and careen out in a wake of considered quiet, to invite which messages hum
    in your head
and which echo back in their own translations, say, as you stop in the hallway
    later at work
to shake a colleague's hand. It is these affirmations that add music to your
    voice,
and surprise you when, looking out from a rooftop over a city with a sense of
    good chance
you almost could not have imagined, you can say "I know I've wanted to be
    here before."

Voice Lessons

All My Exes

All my exes, how I could care less
about your addresses,
your dogs, your daughters,
or the state of your kitchen.

I will live in the secure orbit
of not giving a good god damn
about your prescriptions,
your obsessions,
or the color, this week,
that you are painting your toes.

Family of past loves,
envelop your children
in thy care. Circle your wagons
around them on this night
and kindle a fire of distraction.
Talk of other dates,
other husbands, fiancés, lovers, friends.

But when the conversation
comes around to me
and the sharp barbs have pierced the skin
of the old stories
associated with my name,
please discourage them
from seeking me out
among the vastness of everybody else.

Direct, instead, their attention
to some other someone else.
Entreat them to extend that choice phrase
that they might have reserved for me

to their new friends and potential exes.

Get them away from me!
I have a wife to have my coffee with
in the morning. I have her name
to address my letters to,
her jeans to pick up off the carpet
when I come home.

Voice Lessons

Mixed Up Weather

Twelve feet of snow in Milwaukee this morning
and here, two time zones away,
seventy degrees and bright,
a slight wind swaying the eucalyptus.
This faux-fall here in Arizona the weather gets all mixed up,
doesn't know if it wants to be spring, or winter, or fall.

Other years, I'd be on bicycle
grooving to the chill, our five months reward;
helmet webbing strapped under my chin
feet circling in the stirrups,
but this new season I'm content to round the corner
at the speed that four dachshund feet can lead.
We get to the very edge of the park and bolt
through the leaves crisply hushing under our feet
as we run through the obstacle course of trashcans and trees.

And I keep a wide distance from the pond, this man-made
depression that passes for a lake in these parts.
I see the pond's sole, dusty heron, like some Victorian contraption
that you would check by the coat rack in some brownstone's foyer.
I don't want to startle, send into flight, this bit of antiquity
during its quiet vigil over the meager crappies and catfish
that daily attract the bird to our neighborhood lake.

The poet John Logan talks about how, after three moves in six months,
he still remained the same, about his similar suburban shore
and its lame ducks, drunk on the swill from boats.
I see the same complacent clucks. But who says they have to fly...

Who says you can't walk reverently around a rare experience?
That you can't sneak up on a singular species,
a change of mode, a change of awareness, a mixed-up season?

At home, the Christmas lights are on,
a string of fireflies under the eaves.
Wrapping paper is laid out on the table
next to today's festive FedEx delivery.
And I take this chance to speak out in a clear voice for joy,
for what is rare. For what is meant from the soul.

I'll wait. I'll wait it out.
If tomorrow, that dusty heron should be gone,
I'll wait out the ducks.
I'll wait out the ducks till some new mixed season comes along
that leads me to song, that frees me from the dry words of work
and gives me ease of mind and voice.

Voice Lessons

A Golden Solution

What started as mathematical calculations run amok,
Archimedes, vexed by an elusive solution
to the king's weight in gold, was asked by his wife to rest –
to take a bath.

And how the king's weight displaced not so much gold,
but a golden solution in so many moments' peace.

This is a recipe for weekends. This laying back.
This is a recipe for weekends, I think, as I relax in the hammock
    with an eight week old dachshund resting on my chest,
      a paperweight of pure, puppy affection;
        trading, between us, a long, quiet diet of heartbeats.

And while looking out across the backyards of my block,
I think of some, as yet unformed metaphor
perhaps the utility lines strung on poles along our properties' borders
which connect us all in some old-timey way
and the bath that I'm taking, filled with the dusty scent of warm grass
and the sounds of birds filling up the space,
like a large languid bath of blue sky and a tranquil mind.

Dog Among Icons

The collages of Tony Fitzpatrick litter the page with 1950's cigar box art – advertising icons of sex and culture and commerce. Naked figures holding bubbles. Saints with halos and robes. Hotel and dance hall matchbook covers signify a Chicago convinced of its own mid-century importance. And at the center of some of these adult, visual equivalents of the old cigar box where my grandmother kept buttons and trinkets meant to captivate the imagination of her grandkids on weekend visits… Dogs!

Dogs in all their oblivious self-possession. Dog as blues hound. Dog as Egyptian god of the dead. Dog as constellation. Dog as flowered, psychedelic wonder. Exalted dog! Exuberant dog! Dog that burns through the negative emulsion of the world like a hot brand!

And that's how I feel about being the owner of a dog here in the center of my late-century home littered with stuffed animals with gnawed-down ears, dragged-in eucalyptus leaves, snapped branches and frayed pine cones strewn across the diffuse highlights of our hardwood floor as Rigatoni, dog of curious, constant agitation; dog-master of the rubber squeaky toy; dog of purposeful attentiveness; dog of ounce per ounce explosive love, leans, in this rare, quiet minute between barking at birds and running after toys, to rest upon my bare feet as I type.

Voice Lessons

Exchange of Devotion

Blessed splintered bone of dog
They had to grind you in flames
till your limbs snapped
They had to make you abstract
They placed you in a box of black plastic
Flecks of tooth and marrow
dust of flesh and eyelash
slipped in Ziploc skin
to seal you from the living

I place you – a heap of moon
under an oval stone
A bowl of milk
laid at the level of roots
A dozen fistfuls of dust displaced
to make your desert grave
in a place you would have loved
lizards and holes
fragrant with the scent of den

I sit in the silt, to lean
close to you
recalling
how when you licked my face
you'd hook
your tooth against my skin
a feral nip
that ripples through me still
And I feel
when I press
my hand to your stone
like a dog at the heels of its master

About Face

It's tough to track the face.
Tough to monitor the visage
aside from posing
in the mirror for a minute.
And always you come to this proscenium,
wondering if your features have shifted.
Look around – no face here.
Arms and legs, belly and breast, plus
any accoutrement you might, then, possess.

Try to steal a glance.
can you catch a trace –
a smudge of nose, or lip, or chin?
But don't give in.

Your face has a purpose beyond appearance.
Sometimes, the sounds of words take precedence.
Other days, I bet it's the text
those words purport to represent.
Often, the space above the neck
seems a duct or vent,
to aspirate whatever emotion
crept under the hair to take residence.

I wonder how the average Hank can handle it.
Looking back on the line at the bank
I see a pantomime of paradox,
a gallery of mystery.

It's as if the body were a stalk
for a blossom of terrible transparency.

Voice Lessons

The Poem as Conduit

Let me be direct,
this isn't a case of status.
There's no monetary incentive,
just a plain overtime with words
worried over enough to be personal
and considered, or not, like advice.

No need to be adversarial!
Some statements hit the mark, others miss directly.
It's not like I've hired any personnel,
given some adjunct poet quality assurance status
over these measured moments of words;
although I did try to be inventive.

After all, your respect is incentive
enough to take under advisement
as I wrench around these words
according to a set of mathematical directions
(thought by some, in the Middle Ages, to have numerological status)
while trying to make the formal, personal.

It may be that even the most mundane memos are personal.
Simply asserting the self is enough incentive
to give the most hopeless poem some status.
And after a few lines, the poem seems to advise
itself, takes its own direction,
forms its own thoughts, in its own words.

Think of the poet as psychic, as a conduit for words
that simply leap out of the lexicon to be their own person.
Who am I to impose direction
on words whose desire to be heard is their sole incentive?
Insolent, they breeze past my advice

and take their place on the page like heads of state.

They raise their serif'd fists at me and state
in words as plain as words
their sound advice
that I, mistakenly, attribute to my person;
falsely claim as my own insight,
when, indeed, language plays through me directly.

The status of my name on this page is incidental.
Words are mystical. They're interpersonal.
Any advice you take from this page, you take from language directly.

Most of the end words were taken from a pay stub, as inspired by a poem by Ruth Hulbert who chose, as end words for her sestina, disciplines from a previous semester's class schedule.

Voice Lessons

Certain Counsel

The verdict is still out
    on The Beginning – Day One,
    was it? Where matter
    found a loophole in The Word
    and begot Light.

For all its powers, was that start-up, Gravity
    overvalued at its IPO
    and, given its uncertain return,
    is our current growth just an aimless breeze?

Should we, instead,
    select a different pose,
    a different benchmark
    for which to stack the deck?

Demand only the best
    telepathic blast
    from The Boss Upstairs.
    Or stay at home and play ping pong –
    whatever piques your interest.

I have trouble imagining
    any certain counsel
    on Kingdom Come
Save the bargain meditations found in poems
    that pull no punches, and plainly
    reset the gaps in our perceptions
    like psalms discovered in child's play.

The strength, speed, energy manipulation
    and creation powers available to you

with these resources will allow you
to perceive things on a multi-dimensional level
impervious to the unhappy and difficult minded.

If you find these ground rules attractive,
    please write in
    any notebook or scratch pad
    for at least a fortnight
    and your words will transmute
    and thrive.

Voice Lessons

Love is the Soul of Genius

Love is the soul of genius
in everything, a crazy, shaking, joy
like the cusp of a kiss
like jasmine before a storm

In everything, a crazy, shaking, joy
plays me like a medieval instrument
like jasmine before a storm
I lift the petals to my face

they play me like a medieval instrument
Plucked, like some bright harpsichord
I lift these petals to my face
and laughter shatters the mundane

Plucked, like some bright harpsichord
I call out your name
and laughter shatters the mundane
in an invitation of all-directed joy

I call out your name
but you refuse, suspect, decline
this invitation of all-directed joy
choose, instead, your fearful thoughts

Where you refuse, suspect, decline
I accept, imagine, embrace
change, instead, those fearful thoughts
to synesthetic, sensual, play

To accept, imagine, and embrace
like the cusp of a kiss
To know, in synesthetic, sensual, play
love is the soul of genius.

A Poem for Our Futures

There are many without driving ambition.
There are many to whom ambition comes first.
And some say their life has been happy.
And some say their life has been sad.
And some say their life has fallen markedly short
of the path that would lead to their dreams.

At the start, we have time for our future.
We have time, time enough, for our dreams.
We have time for asides
and for just one more try.
We have time for the next big idea.

Oh, we thought of ourselves as young.
We thought of ourselves as young for so long.
Our future had yet to have passed.

But like many of us, oh, like many of us,
how startled we were at the loss of that promise,
that infinite future that bolstered our dreams.

At some nagging point, our promise had stalled.
At some point, our future had come.
At some point our future had come and had gone,
and our ambition held less and less sway.

And this came for those who were happy.
And this came for those who were sad.
And this came for those who did all that they dreamed.
Came for those far off some longed-for path.

Voice Lessons

Down On Weighted Knees

There was no chalice, no wine or incense
there was no back-lit lamb or splintered saint
no ordained priest in pressed white vestment
when I went on my weighted knees to pray

When I went on my weighted knees to pray
I bent my forehead down towards the ground
and cupped my hands around my prideful face
as one would cup a fledgling that they'd found

As one would cup a fledgling that they'd found
as one would span their hands around a flame
to shield it from the wind that tries to drown
the breath of simple things and simple ways

For breath of simple things and simple ways
I bent down on my weighted knees to pray.

Prayer for Our Parents

My mom, like the sleeping Jesus
of the Pietà, her head to one side
makes us turn, her husband and son, to see,
and for a second, I thought she had died.

There with the daily news laid aside,
stalled the half-breath of thought we would not speak
which my father's pizzicato laugh belied;
and when she moved, it was like a reprieve.

Take now, your parents' hands, before they leave;
like a link in a chain of lives to lives.
And speak from that place of urgency
where any moment may fall short of time.

Voice Lessons

206 Mill Street

Nothing is left of the three-story brownstone
except a book with our birthdays,
and two worn rosaries.

Nothing remains of the repainted doors;
the sculpted moldings with their corner florets
couldn't keep them in their frames.

The painted, ceramic curios have left their doilied stage
taking with them the black tricycle,
and a cigar box of marbles, some jacks, and a dreidel.

The Dynaphone Victrola and the Caruso 78's weren't that long in leaving.
The avocado pit suspended over water did the last Houdini.
And Saint Anthony, through some sly ascension, sits in pawn,
along with the shellacked box that I made in wood shop.

Gone the grape arbor, the tomato garden,
and the pear tree that spread its fruit upon the lawn.
The rust red spigot wheezed and brought up dust.
And the parsley sprigs peering along the walk
have withered, and are gone.

Nothing's left of the three-story brownstone
except a book with our birthdays,
and two worn rosaries.

Music Appreciation

My aunt Faye had a mausoleum of a piano
which was wedged in the hall like an architectural member.
Dust whirled in the air around its casement
like dancers at an old-world festival.

Faye would play with what seemed to be her knuckles
an arthritic rendition of "Back to Sorento"
or a rusty old aire that memory lent her
while Sam, her husband, hammered
down in the basement.

What he did in the cellar – he wouldn't tell her,
but when the music would flow, he went below
to work out his temper.

Voice Lessons

Madam Goldfuss accompanied us
on an out of tune piano.
Her mixed class consisted of
myself, a snowbird from Manhattan,
and a part-time secretary.

Bridgette sang a German Lied,
Mary loved Vaccai,
I was wrestling with a tenor's voice,
and the Madam thought the world of Streisand.

Madam Goldfuss had a pedagogy
that evolved from years of practice:
it went: You can never encourage enough.
It doesn't hurt to schmaltz it up.
And any song can be made more crucial
if you have some love behind the voice –
so why not match your students up.

Yes, and it was love that fueled their songs,
as the wily Madam winked:
"Come closer dear, let's you and the boy sing together."
Such scales would make a master wince.

Sure enough, this worked for a bit,
the secretary and I
loosening up our vocal chords
and sometimes letting slip
a telling glance
on the parts where we didn't have to try.

But somehow something happened

after I found a new girlfriend.
While I still love Gigli, Caruso, and Martinelli,
when we sing it's with such unvarnished delight
that there's no need coax us
into another reckless chorus
of some bubble-gum Beatles theme
while we're naked in the bath.

Voice Lessons

My Papy's Hand

My grandfather's shoe shine kit
was his compass – told him
where he was, on a corner
in Little Italy – its sides knocked together
from broken boards and nails scrounged in the street.
It was a shellacked, Guinea-green
with a red "10 cent" smeared on its face
in my Papy's hand.

He'd kick the living shit
out of any mick
fool enough to claim *his* space
along the morning's route.
He'd built a brownstone
by the time I'd known him
brick by brick with fingers and
hands as rough as rasps.

It made him spit
to see me, in platform shoes and lime green pin-stripe pants,
a dandy, and self-professed pacifist by the age of six;
with nothing to hold me to any one place or history.

To him, I was just polite talk and a foolish grin;
looking for a description that would connect me,
through some book I was reading, to a world
I could have seen
clear enough had I simply worked,
and stood my ground
on a corner of the world he'd wedged us in.

Our Last Defiant Days

A whirl of world turned on when I was born.
Lava lamps, love beads, the Vietnam war,
The Graduate, *2001*, and LOVE
had ran their run, while Uncle Ed had left
again without his stash of Gordon's gin.

FM pushed the 45 all the way
to oblivion of chrome and vinyl
pried off the walls and floors so orange shag
could root in mossy groves of earth tones.

Jacked-up vans made tracks upon the communes,
as Dickie-boy sweat out his own disgrace.
It seemed the global poles had mildly turned
to thoughts of satellite and microwave.

We learned that Uncle Ed left for the city.
He fought in bars and joined the IRA.
While in the sky they do-si-do'd technology
which sent back snapshots of our license plates.

Voice Lessons

The End of Mischief

What mechanism of the nineteen fifties
caused my father to turn away from the prankish tale,
the mischievous act with no bad intention;
the times he laid to wait on the fire escape of a tenement?

What pen in pocket like some new harvest
was made to replace the bar-stool antic, or the dare
for his brother to jump into the pit and put a penny on the tracks?

Was it my Mom's religion that caused my father to trade-in
his leather jacket for an account at the credit union?
Was it my uncle's drinking, or the way he maneuvered
the hind end of a hook-and-ladder into an office building?

Was it technology with its oscilloscope
that gave my father new insight into the beating of his heart?

When did he turn away from the laxative in the coffee,
an impulse only to surface on Saint Patty's Day with a mock sneeze,
a hand to his nose, dangling a strand of fat from a slice of corned
    beef?

Or was it in Korea, as he told me, the time he was drunk in the
    street
where women waited to stone him should he open his car door
to drive back to the base? There, where the Navy ship-man as-
    phyxiated
on the floor of the U.S.O. from whiskey fumes rising in his throat.

Did all this quell his puck-like desire?
No more mannequins dropped from the rooftop?
No more bets with the Swede to kiss a ten-pound sledge?

Or was it me?
Was it something about his son that he could not trust
to bad behavior? The adolescent bootlegging on the hill
squelched before the sun had set,
the blackberry juice scorched to the aluminum pot, barely cooled.

Was it something of my decade? Was he scared
by the riots in Detroit, or by the assassination of too many
good Democrats during the decade after I was born?

What was it that made him trade in his leather jacket?
What made him sell that black Indian motorbike?

Voice Lessons

The Leader

All summer, through the sunlit-emerald, Iroquois woods
we moved like ticks, unseen among the Boy Scout green.

The gilt stitched patches appeared as wounds
on our shoulders and ribs, but don't be fooled

Our cruelty was checked by a membrane so thin
it burst, easily, and often.

And as our patrol roamed in want of trouble,
we needed a leader, someone who would give assent

With a nod that clicked like a trigger
and sent us hurling like calves from a pen.

I see it now, like a montage from an infantry movie;
the new recruits storming the barracks, already transformed by war,

While half-visible in overlay, the leader, his lips
angled in disdain, yelling, "get them!"

And I can see as we skipped paddles onto the lake,
and cut loose canoes from their pontoon

That he wasn't entirely mean or bad. Our leader, Joey Carbino,
whose name echoed, eerily, of carbine.

His glasses were a Sprite bottle green
and his left, drifting eye belied a passive demeanor.

I could tell, even as he whipped my legs with a halved sapling,
even as he dubbed me Rockhead,

That he tried, in his own militant way,
to exact perfection.

And he knew the point upon which our actions turned
was laughter; and *that* oil was what he would use

to make the taunts and slapstick seem natural.

Voice Lessons

All Our Soiled Laundry

There were ponies prancing on the mattress
in the smallest bedroom of the home,
worn show horses not meant to embarrass,

unthought secrets no guest could ever guess –
the unkind details you'd expect from a poem.
Like the blurred roan ponies on the mattress

that moved about our dreams like Pegasus
leaving dark marks we quickly disowned
since to show them would only embarrass.

On the bed's white thread the horses grazed
like migrant hands on private clothes,
shirts rubbed open like sheets on a mattress.

Each untold act of our adolescence
where something in our touch
failed to convey a human embrace

now leaves us in our homes, alone and laughed at –
rubbing bruises we never hoped to own.
There are ponies prancing on the mattress,
worn show horses not meant to embarrass.

Two Statues

They do not break for scones,
they do not scratch inside their ears.

Their jaws are as taut as suspension wires.
They haven't laughed in years.

They do not smile, they show no dread;
they're outtakes from the School of David.

But for all their formulaic, idealized beauty
I'm sad, for they have never seen a movie,

or cheered a lively hockey game,
or smoked a pipe – they resist change.

These guys, they simply lack some flair:
the thing a Hawaiian shirt might repair.

Voice Lessons

What Hollywood Wants from a Poem

Where is the formula, we ask.
Where is the formula?
We've searched
through your past
loves and embarrassments
scrutinized your habits
and now we're closing
in on your vice.
After all, we have
ways of making you talk.

You've cooperated so far,
we tell you, thanks for the couplet,
the instance of rhyme,
your diaphanous diction,
the clever jive of your tongue.
But now, it's beyond all that patter;
(Don't listen to Pater!)
it isn't toward music we aspire.
It's the formula:
how to make it fly,
how to have it come together
and bind us
in some kind of human
understanding;

let's join hands.
Oh yes, the sky,
very nice,
and the adjectival lawn
that appears to be so strong
under our feet.
Let's put it more in the present.

Let's give it
real appeal,
Whitman meets Scorsese,
Dickinson at "The Piano."
Who cares?
As long as it sells.

Look at your brother;
his simple success.
What did it take for him to invest
in a launderette?

And after two years
of soap
he's got himself
a boat
and a home:
what it takes
to belong.

So, I'm speaking to you
as a cautionary voice.
We'd like something
that rises past
the usual standards;
something a little more.
Something that talks back:
to put it plain,
a poem
that kicks ass.

John Tynan received his MFA in creative writing from the University of Arizona in 1997. In addition to writing poems and stories, he also composes songs and plays the accordion. He currently lives in Beijing, China, where his wife Rene Gutel is a diplomat for the U.S. Department of State, and makes his living as a web developer.